# JOHNNY'S BIRTHDAY SURPRISE

## A CHILDREN'S BOOK BY:

# MARSHALETTE R. WISE

verbs
Johnny's Birthday Surprise
Shhhh!!!! It's a secret!!
Written by: Marshalette R. Wise

# WISE Scholars Publishing
## "We Bring LIFE to LEARNING"

First published by WISE Scholars Publishing, May 2012
Atlanta, Georgia, USA



10    9    8    7    6    5    4    3    2    1

**www.wisescholarspublishing.com**

Library of Congress Cataloging-in-Publication Data

Wise, Marshalette R.
*Johnny's Birthday Surprise: Shhhh!!!! It's a secret!!*

**Paperback**
ISBN-10: 0615673007
ISBN-13: 978-0-615-67300-4

**Hardback**
ISBN-10: 0-9963946-3-X
ISBN 13: 978-0-9963946-3-5

Printed in the United States of America



**DISCLAIMER:** This is a work of fiction. Names, characters, businesses, places, events, and incidents are either the products of the author's imagination or used in a fictitious manner. Any resemblance to actual persons, living or dead, or actual events is purely coincidental.

Johnny wakes up and throws his sheets.
He can't wait to open his treats.
Johnny jumps high into the air,
Then suddenly begins to stare.

He sees his red shirt on the door,
And quickly glides across the floor.
Johnny doesn't even make his bed.
He goes to eat breakfast instead.

As Johnny combs his woolly hair,
He slides down the side of the stairs.
Today is Johnny's eighth birthday.
What will his dear family say?

Holding pancakes cooked golden-brown,
His mom says, "Johnny… please get down!"
His sister thcn complains and begs.
She says, "I don't want any eggs."

His mom says, "Sit down and let's eat."
Johnny just frowns and takes a seat.
He looks side-to-side then around.
No cards, gifts, or balloons are found.

Johnny can't smile although he tries.
"Pay me some attention," he cries.
As his sister silently chewed,
His mom began to eat her food.

He thinks, "Where's my birthday wishes?"
His mom says, "After school… wash dishes."
He then sighs and throws up his hands.
His mom says, "And all the pots and pans!"

His sister cuts her food in half.
She looks down and tries not to laugh.
She asks, "Can you pass the syrup?"
They eat without another word.

Off to the bus stop, Johnny goes.
He's sure his friend already knows.
Johnny asks, "How are you today?"
Jane nodded, but didn't look his way.

Brad holds his backpack very tight,
And then turns his head to the right.
Johnny suddenly starts to plea.
He asks, "Are you ignoring me?"

11

Johnny sits down in the front row.
He quickly says, "Good morning, Joe."
As three boys talk about soccer,
Joe just bursts out into laughter.

Johnny decides to chat with Lynn.
She begins to smile, blush, and grin.
Johnny says, "It's a special date."
She says, "We have a new classmate."

Who could Johnny go and talk to?
What should Johnny decide to do?
A boy whispers in a friend's ear,
Making sure that Johnny can't hear.

He stands at the doors to the gym.
Kids walk by like they don't see him.
Johnny starts to feel really sad.
He says, "I'll go visit Coach Chad!"

He goes inside and runs around.
Coach Chad just screams, marches, and frowns.
Johnny sprints and sticks out his chest.
Coach Chad says, "This isn't a gym test!"

Faster and faster, he quickly ran.
Coach Chad shouts as loud as he can.
Johnny feels like going to hide.
The coach says, "Go and play outside!"

As his friends have fun at recess,
He thinks, "My birthday is a mess!"
As Johnny mumbles and kicks rocks,
They play Tug-of-War and Hopscotch.

His birthday sure hasn't gone as planned.
He feels like he's in fairyland.
He says, "I have an English quiz,"
"And they forgot what today is!"

**The students hurry out the door.**
**They shout, "We made a perfect score!"**
**Johnny's teacher stands, smiles, and smirks.**
**She says, "Don't forget your homework."**

As he puts his hand to his head,
The last question is slowly read.
Johnny feels like he's on his own.
He completes the quiz and mopes home.

Johnny can smell some cakes baking.
He wonders what kind they're making.
The yummy icing makes him dream,
Of eating a slice with ice cream.

The baker jumps and stumps around.
He juggles two plates like a clown.
He shouts, "… Delivery to make!"
"You can't have any of this cake!"

Johnny is worried and confused.
He's neither happy nor amused.
Johnny sees his neighbor walking.
He goes to her and starts talking.

Mrs. Smith raises her finger.
She says, "Sorry... I can't linger!"
Johnny says, "Today, I turned eight."
Mrs. Smith says, "I'm running late!"

As Johnny walks by the large park,
He sees a dog that turns to bark.
The owner holds and pulls its leash.
Johnny says, "That was scary... SHEESH!"

There's no birthday cards or wishes.
He even has to wash dishes.
As tears begin to fall and drip,
Johnny pouts and pokes out his lip.

As Johnny's house was getting near,
He said, "It'll be better next year!"
Then Johnny's eyes got big and wide,
When he saw his best friends inside.

He felt like he had won a prize,
When he heard voices scream, "Surprise!"
He saw Mrs. Smith and Coach Chad,
With Lynn, Joe, Jane, and even Brad.

They're all playing and having fun.
Johnny smiles and says, "Thanks a ton!"
With a huge grin, both arms he lifts.
He says, "Look at all of my gifts!"

His mom says, "I'll never forget!"
He says, "There was no need to fret!"
They sing, "Happy Birthday to you...."
Johnny's wishes have all come true!

# ACTIVITY BOOK

"We Bring LIFE to LEARNING"

# TABLE OF CONTENTS


READING .......................................... 34-35

WRITING ....................................... 36-37

LISTENING ...................................... 38-39

SPEAKING...................................... 40-41

SPOT THE DIFFERENCES............. 42-43

CROSSWORD PUZZLES .............. 44-45

WORD SEARCHES...................... 46-47

WHICH DOESN'T BELONG .......... 48-49

MAZES ........................................... 50-51

CONNECT THE DOTS ................... 52-53

COLORING ................................... 54-55

ANSWER KEY ............................... 56-58

# READING

**<u>DIRECTIONS</u>: Read the questions and choose
the correct answer.**

1.   What color is Johnny's shirt?

    a. Blue
    b. Green
    c. Red
    d. Orange

2.   Who did Johnny eat breakfast with?

    a. His mother and father
    b. His mother and sister
    c. His brother and sister
    d. His aunt and uncle

3.   What did Jane do when Johnny spoke to her?

    a. She smiled
    b. She jumped
    c. She ran
    d. She nodded

4.   Where did Johnny go to visit Coach Chad?

    a. The gym
    b. The beach
    c. The mall
    d. The classroom

5.   What kind of quiz was Johnny taking?

    a. Science
    b. Social Studies
    c. English
    d. Art

# READING

6.     What's the name of Johnny's neighbor?

       a. Mr. Jones
       b. Mr. Smith
       c. Mrs. Jones
       d. Mrs. Smith

7.     Why didn't Mrs. Smith talk to Johnny?

       a. She was running late
       b. She was sick
       c. She was eating cake
       d. She was walking

8.     Did all of Johnny's wishes come true?

       a. Yes
       b. No
       c. Maybe
       d. Somewhat

9.     Why didn't anyone tell Johnny about his party?

       a. He already knew
       b. They forgot
       c. It was a secret
       d. None of the above

10.    Which word doesn't belong in the group?

       a. Moping
       b. Pouting
       c. Sulking
       d. Smiling

# WRITING

**<u>DIRECTIONS</u>**: Plan your birthday party by following the instructions.

**Make a list of FIVE people to invite to your birthday party.**

1. My best friend

2.

3.

4.

5.

6.

**Make a list of FIVE foods you want to eat at your birthday party.**

1. Cake

2.

3.

4.

5.

6.

# WRITING

**Make a list of FIVE games you want to play at your birthday party.**

1. **Hopscotch**

2.

3.

4.

5.

6.

**Write a letter to invite people to your birthday party.**

**Dear** _______________________ **,**

    **I'm having a birthday on _________ ____, 20___. The time is from ___:00 until ___:00. I really hope you can come because we'll have so much fun.**

    **We'll eat** _______________________________

_______________________________________**.**

    **We'll play** _______________________________

_______________________________________________

_______________________________**.**

                            **Your friend,**

                         _______________________

# LISTENING

**DIRECTIONS:** Read along to the script as you listen to the audio at  http://www.wisescholarspublishing.com/listening-activity-audio--script.html.

(**SCRIPT**: Happy Birthday To You)
Credit: www.esl-lab.com

**Father:** Hi Michael. Happy Birthday! How old are you today?

**Son:** Seven.

**Father:** Alright. Well, let's sing Happy Birthday:

*Happy Birthday to you,*
*Happy Birthday to you,*
*Happy Birthday dear Michael,*
*Happy Birthday to you.*

**Father:** Alright. So what should we do first?

**Son:** How about cake and ice cream?

**Father:** Okay. Well, uh let . . . let's light the candles. Okay, and make a wish! Don't . . . don't tell me.

**Son:** Don't tell you?

**Father:** Yeah, don't tell me. Okay, and go ahead and blow out the candles. Okay, let's cut the cake, and then we can have cake and ice cream. And what do you want to do after the cake and ice cream?

**Son:** Play freeze tag.

**Father:** Now, how do you play tag?

**Son:** Um . . . one person is it, and the person who is it tries to tag everyone [Alright. And then . . .] before I tag someone and then, another person tags me.

**Father:** Oh, wow. And whose coming over later today for your birthday?

**Son:** Well, everyone. Uh, my cousins, all my aunts and grandmas, grandpas.



**freeze (verb):** become cold to the point of changing water to ice
- It was so cold out last night that I thought I was going to freeze to death.

**tag (verb):** touch a player, usually as part of a game
- I tried to get away during the game at the park, but she tagged me on the back, so I was it.

# LISTENING



**DIRECTIONS:** After listening to the audio at http://www.wischol-arspublishing.com/listening-activity-audio--script.html, read the questions and choose the correct answer.

1. **What is the little boy's name?**

   a. Matthew
   b. Michael
   c. Mitchell

2. **How old is the boy turning in the conversation?**

   a. Seven
   b. Eight
   c. Nine

3. **What does he want to do first?**

   a. Play outdoor games
   b. Open presents
   c. Eat cake and ice cream

4. **Which statement is true about the game at the party?**

   a. You have to catch a large ball without dropping it.
   b. You need to chase children around and touch them.
   c. You need to hide somewhere so no one can find you.

5. **Who is coming to the party?**

   a. Aunts, grandparents, and cousins
   b. Grandparents, cousins, and uncles
   c. Friends, cousins, and grandparents

# SPEAKING

**<u>DIRECTIONS</u>**: Discuss the answers to the questions with a parent, teacher, or friend.

1. Do you think it was wrong for Johnny's family, teachers, and friends to keep his birthday party a secret from him? Do you agree or disagree with them? Why or why not?

2. How do you think Johnny felt when he was eating breakfast with his mother and sister? How do you think he felt at school? How did his feelings change once he got home? Explain your answer.

3. What do you think Johnny wished for when he blew out his candles? Explain your answer.

4. What, if anything, do you think Johnny learned? Who or what helped him to learn this lesson? Explain your answer.

5. What's the best birthday you remember? Why was it your best? What did you do? Who was there? Explain your answer?

6. Have you ever kept a secret from one of your friends? Do you think it is okay to sometimes keep secrets? Why or why not?

7. If you could only invite one person to your birthday party, who would it be? Why? What makes this person special? Explain your answer.

8. Many children can't afford to have parties or receive gifts for their birthday. How are Johnny and those children different? How are they the same? What lesson can Johnny learn from them? Explain your answer.

# SPOT THE DIFFERENCES

**DIRECTIONS:** Look at the below picture for about two minutes. Then on the next page, circle the **eight** differences between that picture and this one.

# SPOT THE DIFFERENCES

<u>DIRECTIONS:</u> Circle the **eight** differences you find between this picture and the one on the opposite page.

# CROSSWORD PUZZLE

## ACROSS

1. not on time
5. comes out of eyes when a person is sad
6. a set of steps leading from one floor to another
9. a place where bread and cakes are made or sold
11. a soft frozen dessert
13. to tsay something quietly
15. a sweet liquid used on pancakes
16. move very quickly
18. opposite of inside
19. a rubber bag which is inflated with air
21. a happy or amused facial expression
22. to shout very loudly
25. made from a mixture of flour, fat, eggs, and sugar
26. at the entrance of a room
27. the sound a dog makes

## DOWN

2. to consume food
3. to pause before saying or doing something
4. a short break given at school
7. whole or completely
8. a person who lives next door or very near
10. a period of 365 days
12. to feel bad or gloomy
14. very happy or eager
17. a place where people live
20. to clean with water and soap
23. a place to sit
24. having no one else

**WORD BANK:** YEAR, WASH, TEARS, SYRUP, STAIRS, SMILE, SCREAM, RUSH, RECESS, OUTSIDE, NEIGHBOR, MUMBLE, MOPE, LATE, ICECREAM, HOUSE, HESITATE, EXCITED, EAT, DOOR, CHAIR, CAKE, BARK, BALLOON, BAKERY, ALONE, ALL

# CROSSWORD PUZZLE



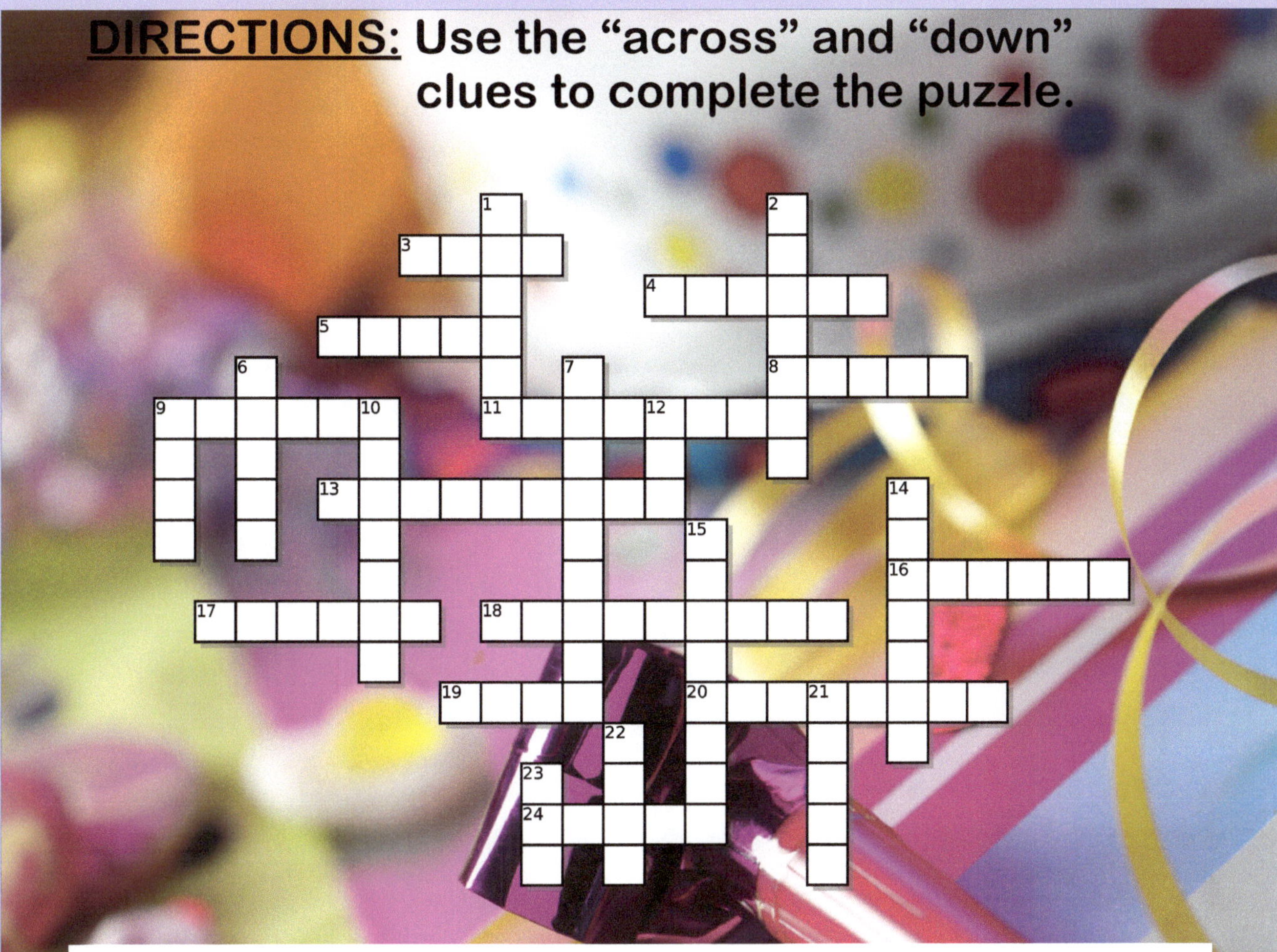

**ACROSS**

3 similar to a test
4 parents and their children
5 a person who teaches an athlete
8 something a person does when upset
9 fail to remember
11 an unexpected event
13 the imaginary home of fairies
16 a place students go to learn
17 a game played by kicking a ball
18 a room in which students are taught
19 a thing given to someone such as a present
20 assignments that a student has to do at home
24 delicious

**DOWN**

1 bowls, plates, glasses, forks, spoons
2 to speak very softly
6 something you win; reward
7 the first meal of the day
9 to be anxious or worried
10 head of the classroom
12 the color of blood or roses
14 a place where a bus regularly stops
15 the day and year a person was born
21 the number after seven; before nine
22 something used to style hair
23 a short word for gymnasium

**WORD BANK:** YUMMY, WHISPER, TEACHER, SURPRISE, SOCCER, SCHOOL, RED, QUIZ, PRIZE, POUTS, HOMEWORK, GYM, GIFT, FRET, FORGET, FAMILY, FAIRYLAND, EIGHT, DISHES, COMB, COACH, CLASSROOM, BUSSTOP, BREAKFAST, BIRTHDAY

# WORD SEARCH

<u>**DIRECTIONS**</u>: Search for the words in blue. Underline or circle each word you find.

```
s  k  g  d  o  w  h  y  a  s  k  i  e  p  k  s  x  g  p  l
i  r  k  i  i  g  a  w  f  n  u  c  a  t  t  m  n  o  a  o
o  t  e  s  f  d  i  r  g  o  r  n  a  e  v  i  g  s  n  o
a  s  h  p  h  t  r  i  o  o  s  e  e  p  n  v  e  r  c  h
e  e  e  t  s  k  s  a  l  l  o  h  y  r  k  i  a  z  a  c
s  t  r  h  s  i  y  h  d  l  s  r  o  l  r  c  h  r  k  s
p  i  v  r  s  t  h  c  e  a  h  m  s  c  l  a  a  b  e  d
b  g  j  f  e  u  a  w  n  b  f  r  e  h  t  o  m  b  s  n
d  a  e  h  a  d  r  i  b  e  i  g  h  t  s  o  u  q  d  e
f  a  v  o  r  i  t  e  r  f  z  i  e  t  c  y  t  a  i  i
g  s  f  o  o  d  r  x  o  s  r  n  r  p  u  r  y  s  s  r
l  f  d  t  i  f  e  s  w  e  t  a  m  s  s  a  l  c  h  f
g  a  i  r  a  q  a  u  n  i  i  c  b  y  w  h  t  m  e  o
c  r  u  m  a  e  t  b  o  g  s  t  o  p  a  m  j  g  s  r
x  h  i  g  z  c  s  n  h  a  r  o  u  n  d  d  y  h  q  l
y  l  e  n  h  s  n  t  p  s  i  s  t  e  r  j  o  z  t  g
y  z  f  w  m  t  e  s  i  r  p  r  u  s  m  u  d  t  i  n
g  y  m  i  e  f  e  r  b  e  x  w  e  i  k  m  o  n  s  f
m  t  l  b  m  d  f  r  c  o  j  h  p  z  u  p  l  i  i  t
t  e  v  p  v  c  g  g  n  m  a  f  u  o  q  s  j  t  v  k
```

| | | | |
|---|---|---|---|
| ahead | cries | hair | sheets |
| around | dishes | jumps | sister |
| attention | eat | laughter | smile |
| backpack | eight | morning | stairs |
| balloons | family | mother | straight |
| birthday | favorite | pancakes | surprise |
| bus | food | pans | syrup |
| cards | friends | pots | today |
| chair | gifts | red | treats |
| chewed | golden-brown | rushes | visit |
| classmate | grin | school | whispers |
| comb | gym | seat | wishes |

# WORD SEARCH

```
p r i z e s q v k b e r o c s r c c k n
s g n i l e e f o v u f b c e h l b r e
s n t p p k p w h v a a h c u a o z o i
k i c i d a l i v s k m e t s l w w w g
r a e r e c q a a e e s u s g y n m e h
i h f d f d u a r g s l r s e t a l m b
m c r s m a e r c s n o i c e e m b o o
s d e l g d s z y t o i o m r d v n h r
h o p s c o t c h m r n m d s l i c e x
s d n a t s i f e y f i y a h h l f z b
v p n y y m o r g u v a c u e i r r y f
j u g g l i n g s s d y i k m r f o f i
d m d o o v s e y r e q t r l m d w z n
r e t t m x d r e r n l a s y e y n r g
w s l w e a t h e r r w b t a l k s g e
m s f i s s c o o u f o e m j t a r g r
m c d e v a t c n o i g s v u q h n a r
g a k i e e k d g h r z t i p m i r d b
z o r t k s r u m o p i n g u c g m l m
p z e c x v t y f r x u n l i y p p a h
```

| | | | |
|---|---|---|---|
| amused | drip | mess | slice |
| baker | fairyland | moping | smiles |
| bark | feelings | mumbles | smirks |
| bowl | finger | neighbor | sorry |
| cakes | forget | perfect | stands |
| chain | frowns | pokes | tasty |
| classroom | happy | prize | teacher |
| clown | homework | questions | test |
| confused | hopscotch | recess | trickle |
| daydream | icing | rocks | tug-of-war |
| delivery | juggling | score | weather |
| dreaming | late | screams | yummy |

# WHICH DOESN'T BELONG?

**DIRECTIONS:** Circle the picture that does **NOT** belong in the group.

# WHICH DOESN'T BELONG?

# JOHNNY'S MAZE

**DIRECTIONS**: Help Johnny and Lynn find their way from the BUS STOP to SCHOOL.

# BAKER'S MAZE

**<u>DIRECTIONS</u>**: Help the **BAKER** find his way from the **BAKERY** to **JOHNNY'S BIRTHDAY PARTY**.

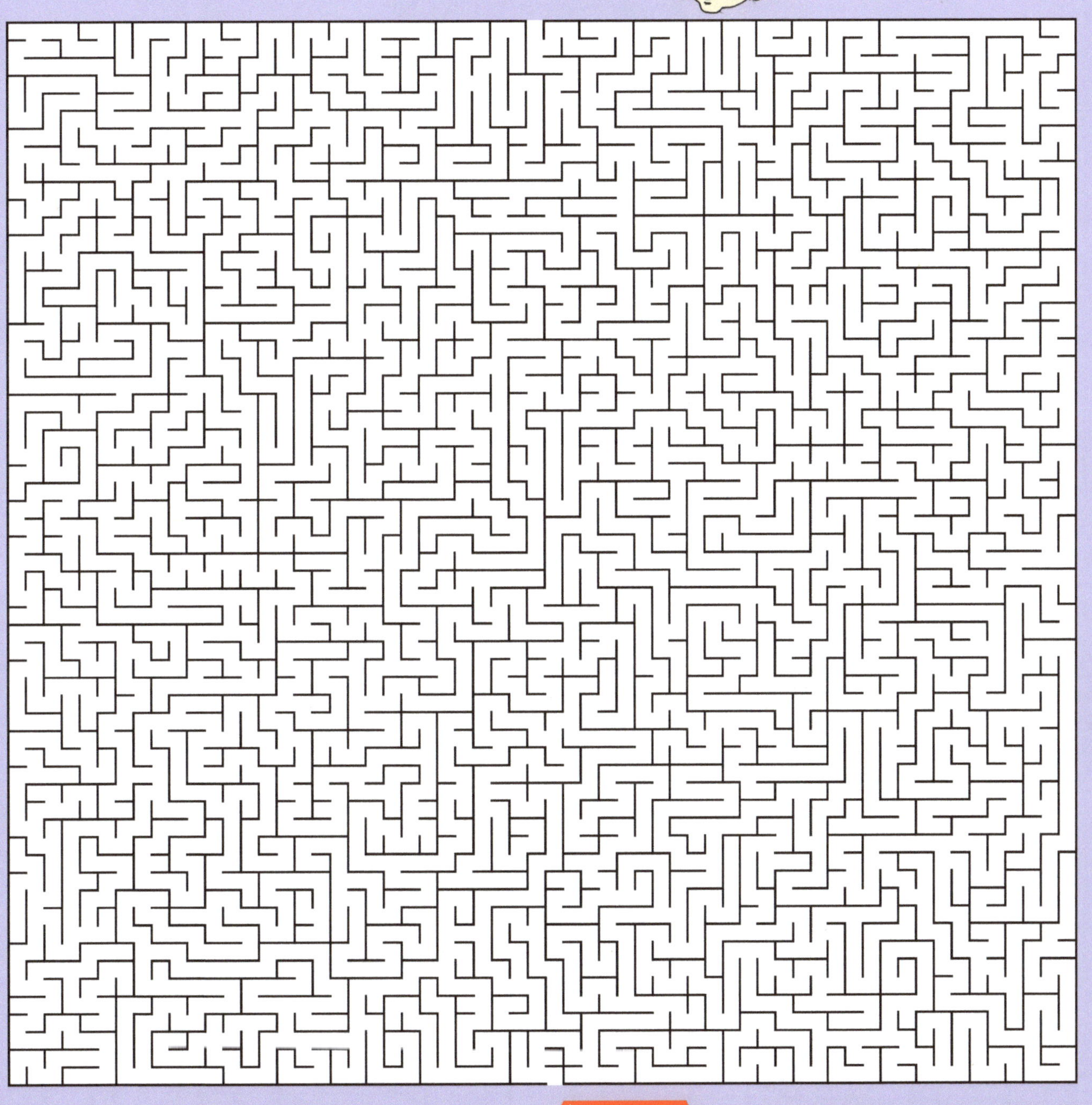

# CONNECT THE DOTS

<u>**DIRECTIONS:**</u> **Connect the dots in the correct number order. You can color in the picture when you are done.**

# CONNECT THE DOTS

# COLORING

**<u>DIRECTIONS:</u>** Color within the lines with crayons or markers.

# COLORING

# ANSWER KEY

**Check your answers to see how many you got right!**

<table>
<tr><td>

### READING

| | |
|---|---|
| 1. | c |
| 2. | b |
| 3. | d |
| 4. | a |
| 5. | c |
| 6. | d |
| 7. | a |
| 8. | a |
| 9. | c |
| 10. | d |

(pages 34-35)

</td><td>

### LISTENING

| | |
|---|---|
| 1. | b |
| 2. | a |
| 3. | c |
| 4. | b |
| 5. | a |

(pages 38-39)

</td></tr>
</table>

## SPOT THE DIFFERENCES

1. The sky out of the window is darker.
2. Lynn's shoes are a different color.
3. Johnny's shirt is a different color.
4. Joe's hair is a different color.
5. Joe's shirt is a different color.
6. The boy is missing his glasses.
7. The boy is now wearing a book bag.
8. One boy is missing.

(pages 42-43)

# CROSSWORD PUZZLES

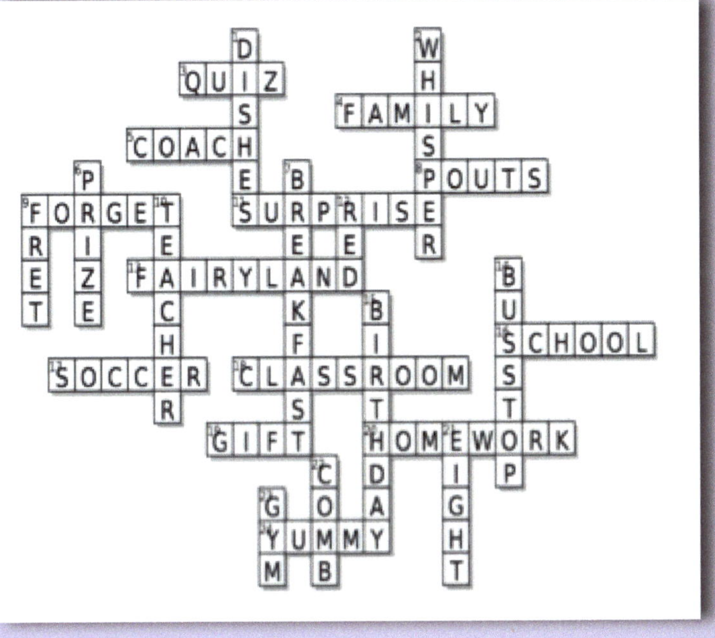

**(pages 44-45)**

# WORD SEARCHES

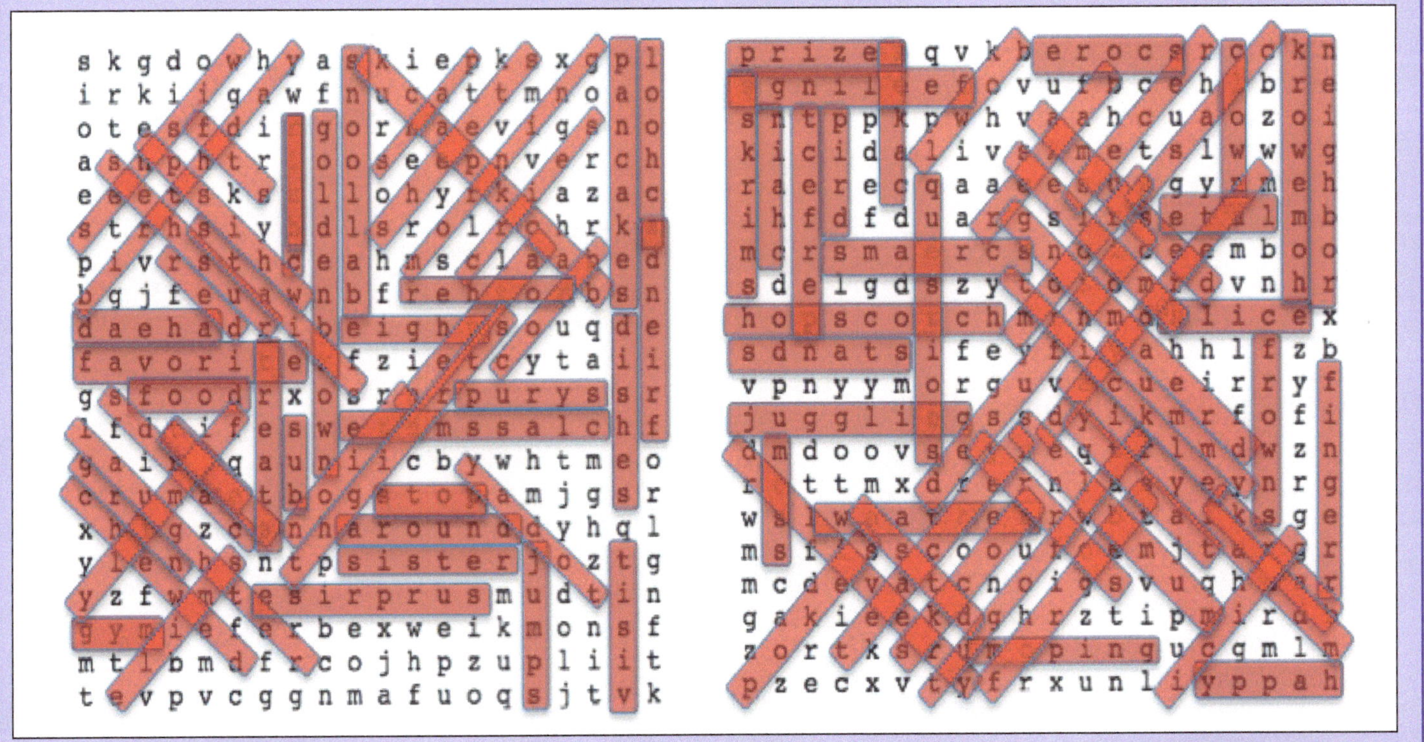

**(pages 46-47)**

# WHICH DOESN'T BELONG?

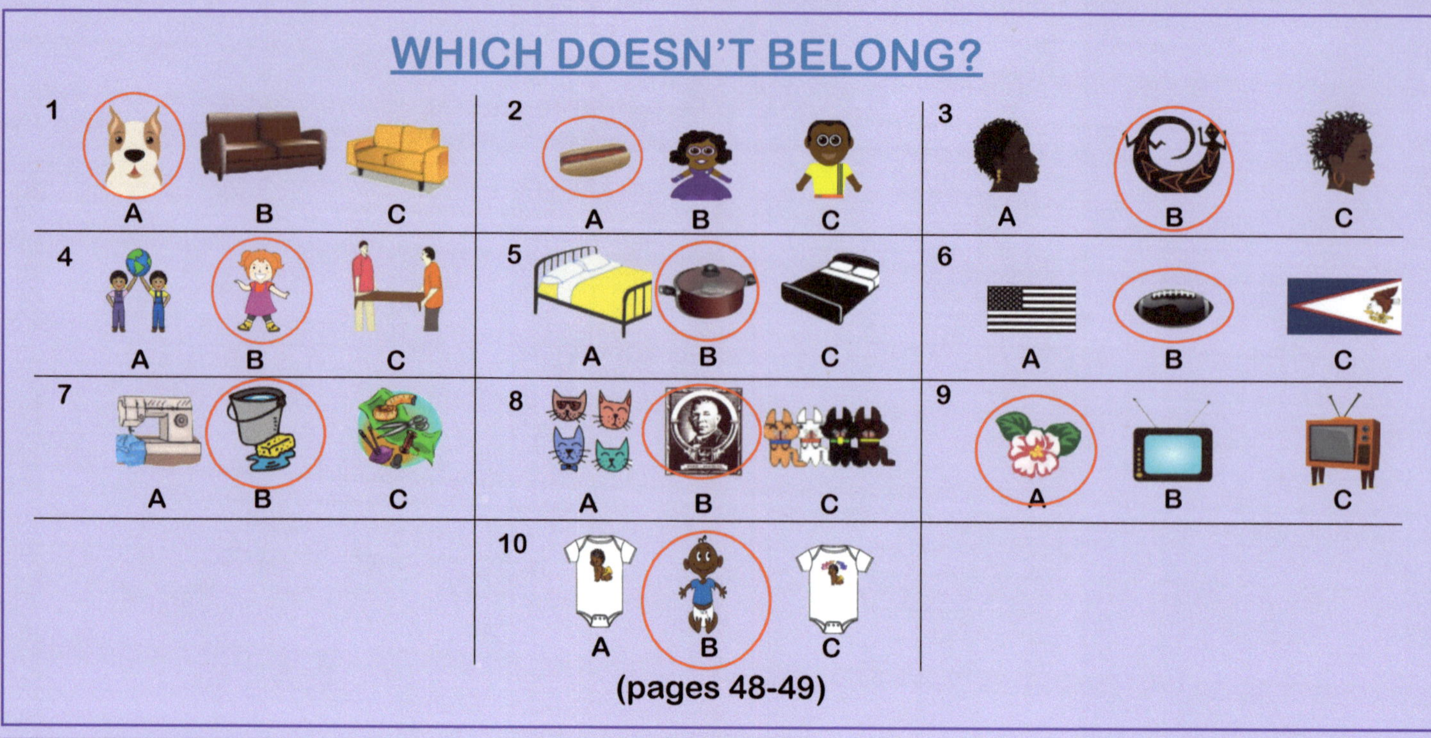

(pages 48-49)

## JOHNNY'S MAZES

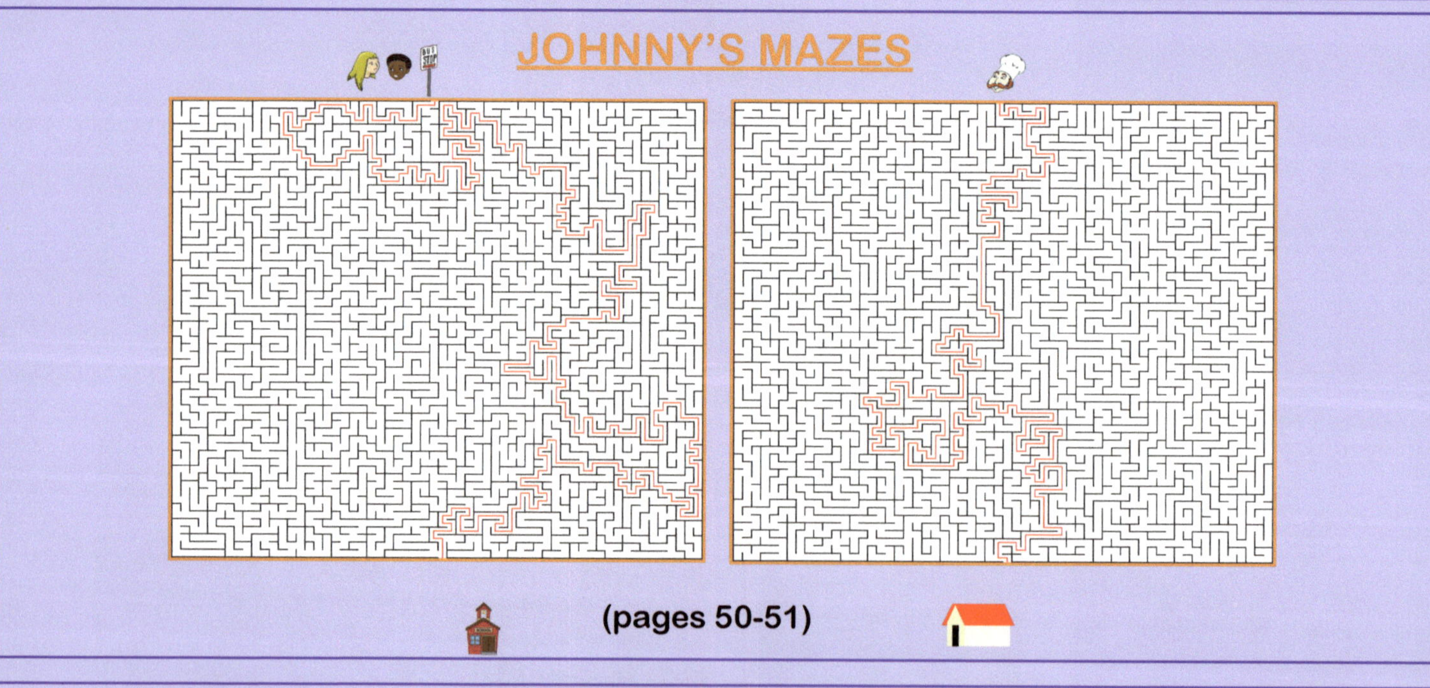

(pages 50-51)

## CONNECT THE DOTS

(pages 52-53)

# We hope you enjoyed reading
## *Johnny's Birthday Surprise….*

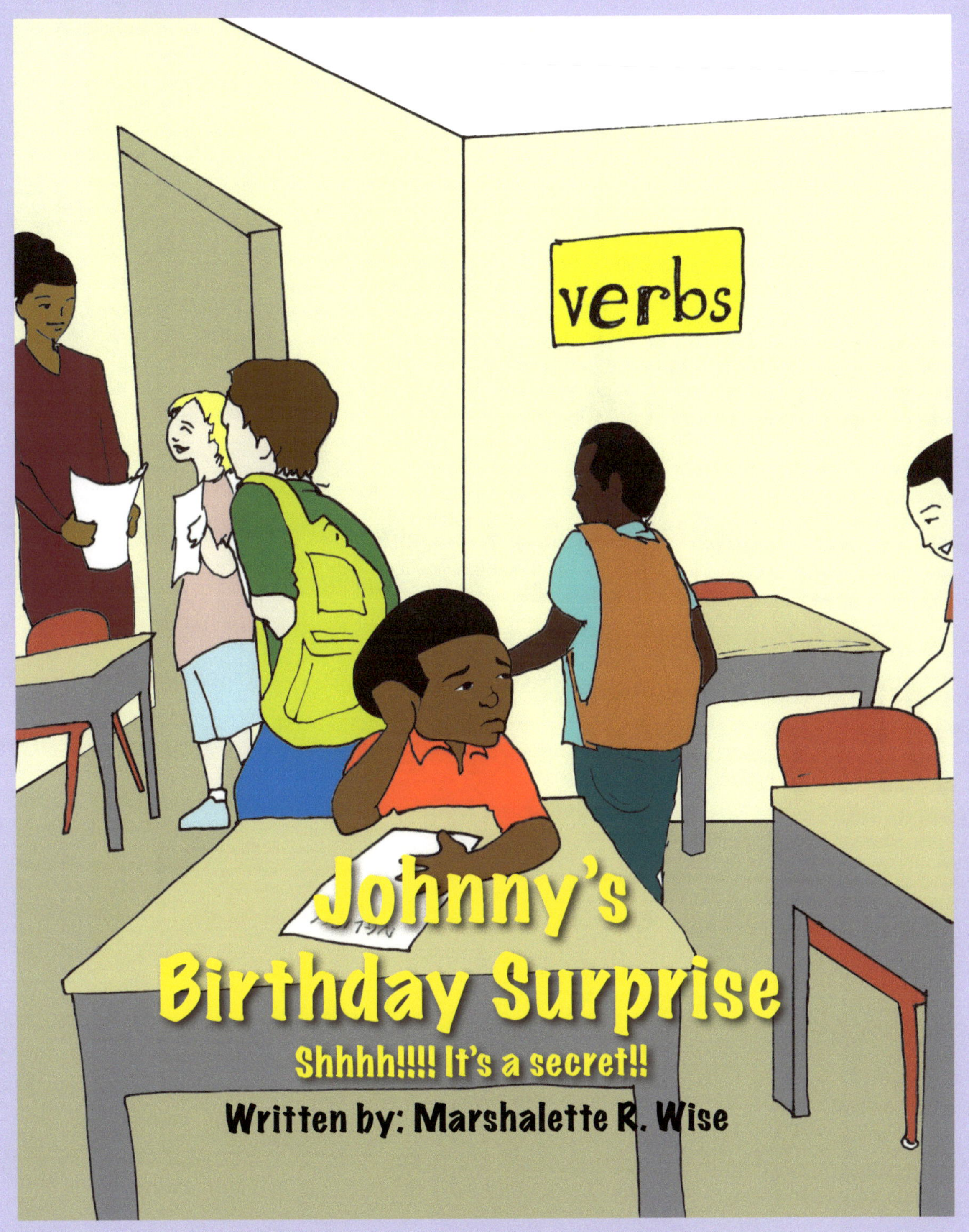



# Turn the pages to view some of our other children's books.

MUCH
HAIRDO
ABOUT
NOTHING
Father-Daughter Dance
written by
Marshalette R. Wise, M.Ed.

# BYE-BYE BIG BULLY

WRITTEN BY
**Marshalette R. Wise, M.Ed.**

ILLUSTRATED BY
**Ronald Scott McDowell**

# CONTACT US

## WISE Scholars Publishing
### "We Bring LIFE to LEARNING"

🌐 www.wisescholarspublishing.com

f www.facebook.com/wisescholarspublishing

📷 wisescholarspublishing

t @marshalettewise

✉ marshalette@wisescholarspublishing.com

☎ 1-888-735-6392

📠 1-334-452-4596 (Fax)